The Mystery of the
Stolen Statue

THIRD-GRADE
DETECTIVES #10

The Mystery of
the Stolen Statue

by
George E. Stanley

illustrated by
Salvatore Murdocca

ALADDIN PAPERBACKS

NEW YORK   LONDON   TORONTO   SYDNEY

First Aladdin Paperbacks edition November 2004

Text copyright © 2004 by George Edward Stanley
Illustrations copyright © 2004 by Salvatore Murdocca

ALADDIN PAPERBACKS
An imprint of Simon & Schuster Children's Publishing Division
1230 Avenue of the Americas, New York, NY 10020

Designed by Lisa Vega
The text of this book was set in 12-point Lino Letter.
Manufactured in the United States of America
22 24 26 28 30 29 27 25 23

Library of Congress Control Number 2004102670
ISBN-13: 978-0-689-86491-9
ISBN-10: 0-689-86491-4

1018 OFF

To Gwen, with all my love

Chapter One

A big yellow bus was parked at the curb in front of the school.

"We have to hurry!" Todd Sloan shouted to Noelle Trocoderro. "The class is going to leave without us!"

"Who cares?" Noelle said. "I'm not interested in seeing a bunch of old paintings and statues."

"Well, I am, Noelle," Todd said. "And I think you will be too when I tell you what I found out last night about art museums."

Noelle stopped walking. *What?* she asked.

"I'll tell you on the bus," Todd said.

"I wish we were going someplace to solve a mystery instead," Noelle complained. "We haven't had a case in so long, I've almost forgotten how to solve one."

Todd grinned. "Well, you never can tell what will happen today," he said mysteriously.

Todd and Noelle's class was called the Third-Grade Detectives. This was because they sometimes helped the police solve local mysteries.

Their teacher, Mr. Merlin, used to be a spy. He gave them secret code clues to help them with their cases.

Mr. Merlin's friend, Dr. Smiley, had a crime lab in the basement of her house. She let the Third-Grade Detectives use it when they needed to look at evidence using a microscope.

It was Dr. Smiley who had suggested that Mr. Merlin take the Third-Grade Detectives to the art museum in the big city thirty miles from where they lived.

Dr. Smiley wanted them to see a life-size plaster statue of Joan of Arc.

It was on loan from a museum in Paris, France. Dr. Smiley said the plaster statue was made in 1456. That meant it was more than five hundred years old.

"This has nothing to do with solving myster- ies," Dr. Smiley had told them, "but I think it's a field trip the whole class will enjoy."

When Todd and Noelle finally reached the bus, all the other Third-Grade Detectives were standing in line on the sidewalk.

Amber Lee Johnson was at the front of the line. "You have to go to the back," she said to Todd and Noelle.

"Why?" Todd asked her.

"Because you're late, and I'm in charge," Amber Lee said.

"Who said so?" Noelle demanded.

"Mr. Merlin!" Amber Lee said. "He told me to take a head count to make sure everyone is here.

"When I'm finished, we can all get on the bus and leave.

"You almost missed my count. You almost didn't get to go."

Amber Lee turned around and started count- ing. "One, two, three, four . . ."

"Why did Mr. Merlin put *her* in charge?" Todd whispered to Noelle.

Amber Lee stopped counting. "I heard that,

Todd Sloan," she said. "Mr. Merlin put me in charge because I'm *cultured*."

"Who told you *that*?" Noelle said.

"My mother," Amber Lee said. "Every night before I go to bed, she makes me listen to classical music and look at famous paintings in a big book she got for her birthday."

Noelle rolled her eyes.

Amber Lee stamped her foot. "Now, see what you did! You made me lose count," she said. "One, two, three, four, five . . ."

"Todd, I don't want to spend the whole day listening to Amber Lee talk about how cultured she is," Noelle whispered. "I may ask Mr. Merlin if I can stay here with the other third-grade class."

"No, don't do that, Noelle," Todd pleaded. "It won't be as much fun if you don't go."

Noelle sighed. "Oh, okay," she said.

Amber Lee finished her count just as Mr. Merlin and Dr. Smiley walked up. "Everyone is here, Mr. Merlin," she said. "We can leave now."

"Thank you, Amber Lee," Mr. Merlin said.

Amber Lee led the Third-Grade Detectives

onto the bus. Todd and Noelle found seats together at the back.

Leon Dennis sat across the aisle from them. "I was going to sit with Amber Lee, but she's sitting with Dr. Smiley," he said sadly. "I don't think she likes me anymore."

"Maybe Amber Lee just wants to plan the next Dr. Smiley Fan Club meeting," Todd said. "Amber Lee is still the president."

"No. Amber Lee is going to talk to her about culture," Leon said. "Amber Lee wants to start a culture club. You can only be a member if you're cultured, like she is."

Noelle sighed. "Nobody cares about mysteries anymore," she said.

"I don't agree, Noelle," Todd said. "We just haven't found one to solve."

"I wish we were going to a police station instead of an art museum," Leon said. "We could find a lot of mysteries there."

"You're right, Leon," Noelle said.

"But that's what I wanted to tell you, Noelle," Todd said. "I saw this program on television last night. It was called *Art Museum Mysteries*."

"*Art Museum Mysteries*?" Noelle asked.

"Yes," Todd said. "Strange things sometimes happen to people who own art, so they give it to museums for safekeeping."

"Oh, yeah!" Noelle said. "Mr. Merlin told us about the owners of the Hope Diamond and the people who took things from King Tut's tomb in Egypt."

Todd nodded. "People also steal things from art museums that police all over the world have to search for.

"It's just one mystery after another!

"So that's why I'm glad we're going to the art museum, Noelle. We may be able to find a mystery to solve after all."

Chapter Two

The school bus stopped in front of a big redbrick building.

"The art museum doesn't open to the public for another hour," Dr. Smiley said, "so we'll have it all to ourselves until then."

"Be sure to thank Dr. Kirk for setting up this special tour for us too," Mr. Merlin added. "She's the director of the museum."

The Third-Grade Detectives stood up and got in line behind Amber Lee. They followed Mr. Merlin and Dr. Smiley off the bus and up the steps of the art museum.

A woman unlocked the front door. She stood aside and let them come in. Todd could tell that she had been crying.

"Is there anything wrong, Dr. Kirk?" Dr. Smiley asked.

Dr. Kirk nodded. "Something awful happened last night," she said. "Thieves broke into the museum and stole the statue of Joan of Arc!"

"Oh, that's terrible!" Dr. Smiley said.

Dr. Kirk sniffed. "Yes, it is! This could ruin our museum's reputation," she said. "And the director of the museum in Paris will be really upset too. The statue can't be replaced."

"Have you notified the police?" Mr. Merlin asked.

"Willie did," Dr. Kirk said. "He's the janitor."

Todd saw Mr. Merlin give Dr. Smiley a funny look.

He had seen Mr. Merlin do that before. It meant he was curious about something. Todd wondered what it was.

"But he told them that we want to keep this as quiet as possible," Dr. Kirk continued. "The company that insured the statue doesn't like a lot of publicity.

"They'll just settle the matter with the museum in Paris, and that'll be the end of it."

"Why doesn't the insurance company want people to know that the statue was stolen?" Todd asked.

"When other art thieves hear about things like this, they think the museum doesn't have good security," Dr. Kirk said. "Sometimes they'll try to rob it too."

Just then a big man came into the room. Todd thought he looked like a professional wrestler.

"Don't forget," the man said. "Let me talk to the police when they get here."

"All right, Willie," Dr. Kirk said.

Willie turned and left the room.

Todd saw Mr. Merlin give Dr. Smiley another funny look.

"I hope you're not disappointed. I know you were looking forward to seeing the statue of Joan of Arc," Dr. Kirk said to the Third-Grade Detectives. "But there are lots of other wonderful things in the museum. So just make yourselves at home."

"I'm sure it will still be a very good field trip," Mr. Merlin said.

The Third-Grade Detectives nodded.

Todd looked at Noelle and grinned. "I told you that art museums were full of mysteries," he said. "We found one right away."

"Do you think we can solve it?" Noelle asked. "We've never solved an *art* mystery before."

"Of course we can solve it," Todd said. "It's still a mystery."

He looked around.

Dr. Smiley and Dr. Kirk were talking to each other. Mr. Merlin was looking at a painting on the wall across the room.

"Let's tell Mr. Merlin that we think this would be a good mystery for the Third-Grade Detectives to solve," Todd said.

Todd and Noelle walked over to him.

Mr. Merlin looked up. "Well, I hope you two aren't disappointed," he said.

"Oh, no!" Todd said. "We want to help Dr. Kirk find the statue!"

"Does she know how many mysteries we've solved?" Noelle asked.

"Well, I'm not sure she does, but maybe we

should wait until the police get here," Mr. Merlin said. "Since we don't live in this town, they may not want our help."

Todd was disappointed, but he said, "Okay."

Mr. Merlin thought for a minute. "Of course, I guess it wouldn't hurt if you two did some private investigating on your own," he said.

Todd and Noelle brightened. Mr. Merlin always had good ideas.

"Just look around to see if there are any clues, in case the police ask you later to help them," Mr. Merlin added. "But remember not to touch anything."

Todd and Noelle started looking around the museum.

They saw the tomb of an Egyptian pharaoh.

They saw the marble steps from the front of a Greek temple.

They saw the statue of a Roman general.

They saw old paintings from Britain, France, and Germany.

But they didn't find any clues that would help solve the mystery.

Suddenly Todd said, "I just thought of something, Noelle. How did the thieves get that statue out of the museum?"

"They probably just carried it out, Todd," Noelle replied.

"But *how*?" Todd persisted. "I haven't seen any broken windows, so they didn't get the statue out that way.

"And the front door wasn't broken when we got here either."

"Maybe they broke in through the *back* door," Noelle said. "Let's check it out."

At the rear of the museum, Todd and Noelle found a door that read EMPLOYEES ONLY.

"Should we go inside?" Noelle asked. "We don't work for the museum."

"It's okay, Noelle," Todd said. "Dr. Kirk said to make ourselves at home, so that means we can look *everywhere* for clues."

Todd opened the door. It was a large storeroom.

Todd and Noelle walked inside and headed toward the back door.

The door was locked.

"That's strange," Todd said. "The windows aren't broken, and all the doors are locked."

Noelle gasped. "The thieves must have had a key!" she said.

Chapter Three

"Let's go tell Mr. Merlin!" Todd said.

But just as he and Noelle got to the door leading back to the museum, they ran into Willie.

"What are you two kids doing back here?" Willie demanded. "Can't you read?"

"Of course we can read!" Noelle said. "We're in the third grade!"

"Well, this sign says 'Employees Only'!" Willie said. "You two aren't employees."

"We didn't mean to do anything wrong," Todd said. "We're just trying to solve the mystery."

Willie narrowed his eyes and looked at them. "What mystery?" he asked.

Noelle gave him a funny look. "The mystery of the stolen statue," she said.

"You kids need to mind your own business,"

Willie said. "The police will take care of this."

Noelle started to say something, but Todd said, "Okay. See you later."

"Why did you interrupt me?" Noelle demanded when they were out of Willie's sight. "I was going to tell him about all the other cases we've solved."

"He's not interested in that, Noelle," Todd said.

"I don't like him at all," Noelle said.

"Me either," Todd said.

Todd and Noelle hurried back through the museum.

They found the rest of the Third-Grade Detectives standing together in a group with Mr. Merlin and Dr. Smiley.

Dr. Kirk was telling them about some French paintings.

"Oh, there you two are!" Dr. Smiley said. "I was wondering where you were."

"We were looking at some of the other things," Todd said. "Noelle and I want to be museum directors when we grow up."

Noelle gave him a strange look.

"Oh, really? Well, I think that's wonderful," Dr. Kirk said. "Why don't you two sit next to me at lunch, and we can talk about that?"

"Okay," Todd said.

"I thought you wanted to be detectives," Amber Lee said. "How can you be a museum director and a detective, too?"

"There are always mysteries in museums, Amber Lee. I saw a program about it on television," Todd said. "This museum has a mystery. *Who stole the statue?* So you can be a museum director and solve mysteries, too."

"Well, then I also want to be a museum director, Dr. Kirk, because I'm the most cultured person in our class," Amber Lee said. "May I sit next to you?"

"I only have two sides," Dr. Kirk told her, "but I'll tell the whole class about my job while we're eating. Is that all right?"

Amber Lee looked disappointed, but she said, "All right."

"When did you decide to become a museum director?" Noelle whispered.

"Just a minute ago," Todd said.

"Well, what makes you think I want to be one?" Noelle said.

"I had to figure out a way for us to sit next to Dr. Kirk at lunch, so we could ask her some questions about the stolen statue," Todd explained. "I thought that you would want to hear what she said too."

"Willie told us to let the police take care of it, Todd," Noelle said.

"But Mr. Merlin said it was okay for us to look for clues," Todd reminded her. "And we have to listen to Mr. Merlin. We don't have to listen to Willie."

Dr. Kirk led the Third-Grade Detectives into the museum dining room. They were each given a boxed lunch.

Todd and Noelle sat down next to Dr. Kirk.

Dr. Kirk told the class how she became a museum director.

First she took a lot of courses in museum studies at the university.

Then she worked at different museums all over the world.

"Did you take any courses on how to solve crimes?" Todd asked.

"No, but I did take a course on how to recognize fake art," Dr. Kirk said.

She talked about that for several minutes.

"I'm happy to say that everything in this museum is real," Dr. Kirk said when she finished.

"What do people do with statues when they steal them?" Amber Lee asked.

"They sell them to crooked art dealers for lots of money," Dr. Kirk said.

"How much money will they make for the statue of Joan of Arc?" Todd asked.

Dr. Kirk smiled. "You'll have to ask the thieves," she said. "I really wouldn't know."

"The Third-Grade Detectives would like to help you solve the mystery of the stolen statue," Noelle said. She looked around the room. "Wouldn't we?"

The rest of the Third-Grade Detectives nodded.

"We're really good, too," Amber Lee said. "We've worked on lots of cases before."

"We'll find the statue for you, Dr. Kirk," Todd

said. "Then that museum in France won't be mad at you."

"Oh, that is so sweet of you, but I couldn't ask you to waste your time doing that," Dr. Kirk said. "You should be outside playing with your little friends and leave the mystery solving to adults."

Noelle made a face at Todd. "She's treating us like babies," she whispered.

"Oh, it wouldn't be a waste of their time," Mr. Merlin spoke up.

"The Third-Grade Detectives learn all kinds of things when they're solving mysteries," Dr. Smiley added.

"No, no, no, I just couldn't," Dr. Kirk said. She stood up. "I wouldn't feel right about it."

Just then, Willie burst into the dining room.

"Dr. Kirk! Dr. Kirk!" he said. "The police are here! They found the stolen statue!"

Chapter Four

Dr. Kirk gasped. "Where was it?"

"In a Dumpster behind a grocery store," Willie said. "But the police said it's broken."

"Oh, dear!" Dr. Kirk said.

"They're bringing the pieces back here," Willie said.

"Todd and I think the thieves got into the museum with a key," Noelle said.

"That's not true!" Willie said.

"Willie's right. How could they?" Dr. Kirk said. "Only Willie and I have keys."

"I told you kids to let the police take care of this," Willie said. "You need to stay out of it."

"But—," Todd started to say.

Mr. Merlin interrupted him with, "Perhaps Willie is right, Todd." He looked him straight in the eye and grinned. "We shouldn't interfere with the investigation unless the local police *ask* us to."

Todd grinned back. He understood. When Mr. Merlin told the police about what all the Third-Grade Detectives had done, they would *ask* them to help!

The door opened and several police officers came into the dining room. Each of them was carrying a cardboard box.

"I'm glad you were on duty, Sergeant Coffee," Dr. Kirk said to the officer in front. "You love art, and you understand what a tragedy this is."

"Yes, ma'am. I think we got all the pieces," Sergeant Coffee said. "Do you have any idea who might have done it?"

"It was probably some of those teenagers who were in here last week," Willie said. "They kept making fun of the statue."

"How did you find the statue so quickly?" Mr. Merlin asked.

"We got an anonymous tip right after Willie called to say it had been stolen," Sergeant Coffee said. He turned back to Dr. Kirk. "Willie said you

needed to keep this as quiet as possible. Is that true?"

"Actually, we don't even want an investigation," Dr. Kirk said. "We wouldn't press charges against the thieves, even if you caught them."

"Well, all right," Sergeant Coffee said.

The police left the museum.

"What will you do with the pieces?" Mr. Merlin asked.

"We'll send them back to Paris so the insurance company can see that the statue was destroyed," Willie said, "and then they can send the money to the museum director there."

For several minutes no one said anything. Then Dr. Smiley said, "I guess we'd better get back on the bus. I'm sure you have a lot of work to do."

"Yes, that's right," Dr. Kirk said. "I need to call the museum in Paris and tell them what happened."

"We can't leave before we see that statue," Todd whispered to Noelle. "It may give us some clues."

"Todd! Mr. Merlin doesn't want us trying to

solve this mystery," Noelle whispered back.

"I think he does, Noelle," Todd said. "I saw the way he looked at Dr. Smiley. He's suspicious about *something*.

"I'm sure he was going to ask the police if we could help, but now there isn't going to be a *police* investigation, so it's all up to the Third-Grade Detectives to solve this mystery!"

Todd turned to Dr. Kirk. "May we look at the statue?" he asked.

"Why would you want to do that?" Dr. Kirk said. "It's not really a statue anymore. It's just pieces of broken plaster."

Todd thought fast. "Well, at least we could say we saw it," he finally said.

Dr. Kirk looked at Dr. Smiley and Mr. Merlin.

Mr. Merlin shrugged and grinned. "What would it hurt?" he asked.

"There's no mystery here, so I don't think that's a good idea," Willie said to Dr. Kirk. "We shouldn't let—"

Dr. Kirk laid a hand on Willie's arm, and he stopped talking.

"Well, okay, if it's that important to you,"

Dr. Kirk said. "I guess there really is a little mystery here for the Third-Grade Detectives after all. *Why would those silly teenagers steal the statue and then break it into a lot of pieces?*"

Dr. Kirk turned to Willie. "Take the boxes into the classroom," she told him.

Everyone followed Willie.

He removed the pieces of the broken statue from the boxes and laid them on one of the long tables.

Todd saw metal rods sticking out from the body where the arms and the legs and the head used to be.

"What are those for?" he asked.

"They help hold the statue together," Dr. Kirk explained. "If they weren't there, the arms and the legs and the head probably wouldn't stay on."

"They're just like bones," Willie added.

"Maybe we could glue the statue back together," Misty Goforth suggested. "I have some really strong glue in my desk at school."

"We sometimes have to do things like that," Dr. Kirk said, "but unfortunately a lot of the pieces of this statue have turned to dust."

The Third-Grade Detectives walked all around the table and looked at the pieces of the broken statue.

Finally Mr. Merlin said, "It's time we got on the bus and headed home."

"I'm so sorry about the statue of Joan of Arc," Dr. Kirk said, "but if you'll come back the day after tomorrow, Willie and I will show you how to make your own plaster statues. It's easy. We do it all the time." She looked at Mr. Merlin. "Would you like to do that? The museum is closed to the public then, so no one would disturb us."

"Please?" the Third-Grade Detectives begged.

"I think that sounds like a good idea," Mr. Merlin said.

Dr. Smiley agreed. The Third-Grade Detectives thanked Dr. Kirk and told her they'd see her in a couple of days.

When they were back on the bus, Mr. Merlin said, "I want the Third-Grade Detectives to solve the mystery of who stole the statue and why they did it."

Todd grinned at Noelle.

"Willie thinks it was those teenagers who

made fun of the statue last week," Amber Lee said. "I think they did it because they aren't cultured, like I am."

"A good detective doesn't just go by what people *think,* Amber Lee," Mr. Merlin said. "He or she looks for *evidence* to prove that someone committed a crime."

Mr. Merlin picked up a big notepad. "Here's a secret code clue to get you started," he said.

He wrote:

L i k e z O O K e y
p l A c e T a b l e
o T h e r H E a d s
a B O u t N e E d S

Chapter Five

"Do you have a pencil and some paper?" Todd asked Noelle.

Noelle shook her head.

Todd didn't know what to do.

Normally Mr. Merlin gave them secret code clues in their classroom.

He wrote them on the chalkboard.

Then the Third-Grade Detectives copied them down.

This was the first time that Mr. Merlin had ever written a secret code clue on a big notepad on a school bus.

"I guess we'll just have to wait until we get back to school," Todd whispered.

"Oh no, Todd! Look!" Noelle said. "Amber Lee

has a notepad and a pencil. She's copying down the secret code clue."

"That means she'll solve it first," Todd said. He raised his hand.

"Yes, Todd?" Mr. Merlin said.

"I don't have anything to write with," Todd said. "Did anybody bring a pencil and a notepad?"

Nobody said anything.

"Amber Lee has a pencil and a notepad," Noelle said. "Could she copy the secret code clue for everybody so that we can work on it on the way home?"

"Amber Lee, would you mind doing that?" Mr. Merlin asked.

"Well, this is a new notepad, and I really hate to waste the paper," Amber Lee said, "but I guess I could."

She gave Todd and Noelle a dirty look.

"Thank you, Amber Lee," Todd said. "Mr. Merlin likes the Third-Grade Detectives to work together, and you're working together."

Amber Lee didn't say anything.

But she started making copies of the secret

code clue for everyone. Finally she finished. She handed Todd and Noelle theirs.

"This is one of the easiest secret code clues that Mr. Merlin has ever given us," Amber Lee told them. "It's just a list of words."

Todd and Noelle looked at the secret code clue again:

L i k e Z o o K e y
P l a c e T a b l e
O t h e r H e a d s
A b o u t N e e d s

"Amber Lee is right, Noelle," Todd said.

"That's probably why Mr. Merlin didn't think we needed to write it down," Noelle said. "He thought we could just remember what the words were."

"'Like,' 'zoo,' 'key,' 'place,' 'table,' 'other,' 'heads,' 'about,' 'needs,'" Todd read. "What does that mean?"

"We probably have to put the words in the right order," Noelle said. "If we do that, we'll solve the mystery."

They studied the words carefully.

"Zoo needs key like other heads place table," Todd said.

"You left out 'about,'" Noelle said.

"It still doesn't mean anything," Todd said. He thought for a minute. "Do you think Mr. Merlin only put the important words in the clue and left out words like 'the' and 'a'?"

"He usually doesn't leave out any words in a clue, Todd," Noelle said. "But maybe he did this time."

Todd and Noelle tried adding "the" and "a" in front of some of the words.

They arranged them in all kinds of order.

Still nothing made sense. Todd could tell that the rest of the Third-Grade Detectives were having trouble too.

"Something's missing here," Todd said to Noelle.

If the Third-Grade Detectives had trouble solving a secret code clue, Mr. Merlin would give the class a hint.

Todd raised his hand. "This is a hard clue, Mr. Merlin," he said. "I think we need some help."

Mr. Merlin frowned. "Are you sure you're looking at it right? You need to pay very close attention to the letters," he said. "But if you haven't solved it by tomorrow morning, I'll give you a hint."

Chapter Six

The next morning, Todd opened his front door just as Noelle started to ring the doorbell.

"Did you solve the secret code clue?" Noelle asked as they headed to school.

Todd shook his head. "My dad and I even used a computer program," he said. "We typed in all of the words, but it just gave us a lot of silly sentences."

When Todd and Noelle got to school, the rest of the Third-Grade Detectives were already in the classroom.

No one else had solved the secret code clue either.

"We really do need a hint, Mr. Merlin," Amber Lee said.

Everyone agreed.

"Well, Amber Lee, did you copy down the secret code clue *exactly* the way I wrote it?" Mr. Merlin asked.

"Yes," Amber Lee said.

Mr. Merlin smiled. "Are you *sure*?" he asked.

Amber Lee blushed. "Well, I didn't want to say anything, Mr. Merlin, but I corrected your spelling."

"What do you mean?" Mr. Merlin asked.

"You're always telling us not to use capital letters in the middle of words," Amber Lee said. "But you had big and little letters all mixed up."

"So you really didn't copy the secret code *exactly* the way I wrote it?" Mr. Merlin said.

Amber Lee shook her head. "No," she said.

Some of the Third-Grade Detectives started grumbling.

"Don't blame Amber Lee," Mr. Merlin said. "After all, she's the only one who brought along a pencil and a notepad."

Amber Lee looked around the room and smiled.

"When Amber Lee corrected my spelling, she

thought she was doing the right thing," Mr. Merlin said.

Amber Lee looked around the room and smiled again.

"She shouldn't have done that, though," Mr. Merlin added, "and you can all learn an important lesson from this too."

Amber Lee stopped smiling.

"When you're solving a mystery, you always have to examine the evidence *exactly* the way you find it," Mr. Merlin said. "You should never tamper with it."

Mr. Merlin went to the chalkboard. He wrote:

```
L i k e z O O K e y
p l A c e T a b l e
o T h e r H E a d s
a B O u t N e E d S
```

"Here's a hint," Mr. Merlin said. *"Capitalize the most important words.* Now I'll let you work on the secret code clue for a few minutes."

"Which words are the most important?" Noelle asked Todd.

Todd looked at the clue. "I think the most important words are 'zoo,' 'key,' 'place,' 'table,' and 'heads,'" he said.

"I do too, Todd," Noelle said, "but the clue still doesn't make sense, even if we capitalize them."

"Wait a minute!" Todd said. "*Only* look at the capital letters."

Noelle looked. "L-O-O-K," she said. She turned to Todd. "*Look!*" she repeated.

"Right!" Todd said. He read the capital letters in the second line. "A-T."

"At!" Noelle said. "The rest of the message is 'the bones.'"

"*Look at the bones!*" Todd said.

He raised his hand. He told Mr. Merlin what the secret code clue was.

"That's right, Todd," Mr. Merlin said. "Now then, what does it mean?"

"I'm not sure," Todd said.

"I know! I know! I know!" Amber Lee shouted. "It means the metal rods in the statue. Willie called them *bones.*"

Todd was annoyed with himself that he

hadn't remembered that, but he was glad they were back on track.

When they went to the art museum tomorrow, the Third-Grade Detectives would look at the "bones" and solve the mystery of who stole and statue—and why.

Chapter Seven

After recess Mr. Merlin said, "It's time for our science lesson. I'm going to tell you all about iron and steel."

Todd hoped he would be able to pay attention. If Mr. Merlin gave them a test, he wanted to get a good grade.

But all he could think of was solving the mystery of the stolen statue.

Todd could hardly wait until the Third-Grade Detectives went back to the art museum the next day so he could look at the bones.

"Iron is one of the most important metals that human beings ever discovered," Mr. Merlin began.

Amber Lee raised her hand. "It wasn't the first, Mr. Merlin," she said. "Gold was the first."

"That's right, Amber Lee," Mr. Merlin said. "People have been using gold for more than eight thousand years."

"Wow!" Leon said. "That's a long time!"

"It certainly is," Mr. Merlin said.

"After gold, human beings discovered copper, silver, lead, tin, and then iron," he continued. "People have used iron for more than thirty-five hundred years.

"At first, human beings got iron from meteors that had landed on Earth.

"After that, they discovered iron *ore*.

"Iron ore is just a rock that has a lot of iron in it.

"This is where most of our iron comes from today.

"A long time ago iron was very expensive to process.

"It was more valuable than gold, and human beings first used iron for jewelry.

"Now it's used for making everything from plows for farming to weapons for war.

"To process iron, you heat the ore in a fire with a lot of charcoal and oxygen.

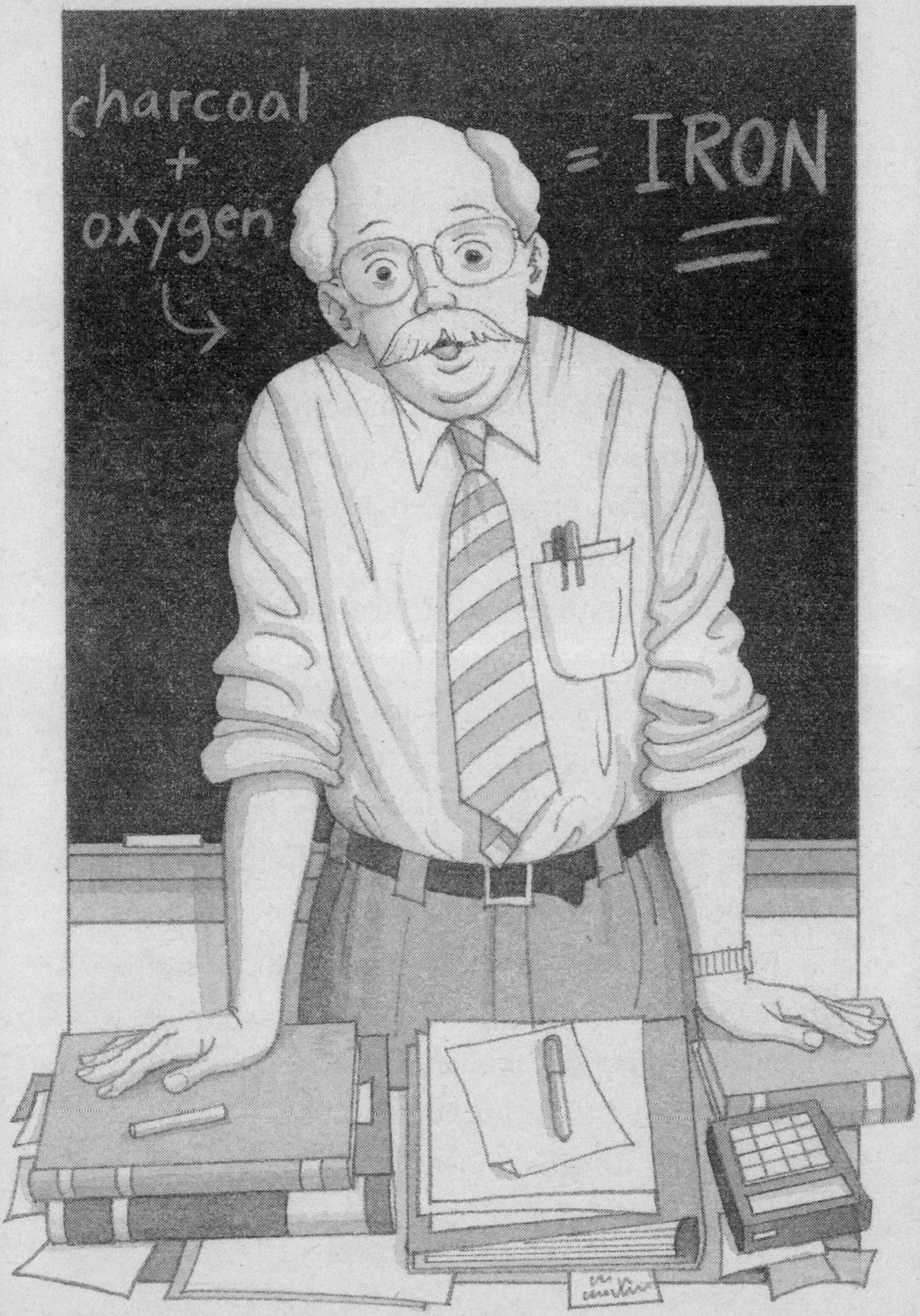
charcoal
+
oxygen
= IRON

"The charcoal combines with the oxygen to make other gases called carbon dioxide and carbon monoxide.

"What's left is a metal called *wrought* iron.

"People use this metal to make tools and horseshoes because when it's heated, they can bend it into whatever shapes they want.

"If you heat iron ore in a blast furnace with charcoal and limestone, you get *pig* iron. Pig iron is used to make steel, which is stronger than iron.

"Steel is iron that has silica, phosphorous, sulfur, and other impurities taken out.

"Over the years, steel has also been processed in several other ways.

"Today, most modern steel plants use what's called the basic oxygen furnace.

"You can test iron and steel in a laboratory and find out what process was used to make them.

"This is the way you can tell how old the metal is."

Mr. Merlin looked at the class. "Any questions?" he asked.

"I'd never wear iron jewelry," Misty said. "I'd only wear gold."

Several Third-Grade Detectives laughed.

"Well, class, Misty has a point," Mr. Merlin said. "Over the years, people wore jewelry made from whatever was the most expensive metal at the time."

"You mean people actually wore *tin* necklaces?" Amber Lee said.

Mr. Merlin nodded.

Leon leaned over to Todd. "I know what I'm going to give Amber Lee for her birthday," he said. "A necklace made out of tin cans."

"Tin isn't a very expensive metal anymore, Leon," Todd said. "You should probably think about giving her something else."

For the rest of the day, the Third-Grade Detectives worked on their spelling, their social studies, and their math.

That night Todd's parents took him and Noelle to an exciting movie at the theater in the mall.

It was about scientists who discovered some old bones in a cave in South America. They spent the entire movie trying to find out where the bones came from.

Right before the end, the scientists solved the mystery. It was a big surprise. The bones belonged to aliens from outer space!

When I get to the art museum tomorrow, Todd thought, *I'll study the bones of the statue, just like those scientists did.*

But he suddenly wondered if he and the rest of the Third-Grade Detectives were in for a big surprise too.

Chapter Eight

The next morning the Third-Grade Detectives rode the school bus back to the art museum.

Dr. Smiley couldn't go because she was busy doing some police work.

Dr. Kirk was waiting for them at the door. "Are you ready to make some plaster statues?" she asked.

Everyone shouted, "Yes!"

"The first thing I'm going to do is look in those cardboard boxes," Todd whispered to Noelle.

When the Third-Grade Detectives got to the classroom, they gathered around the long tables.

Dr. Kirk had put out a small statue mold and some small metal rods for each person.

Todd didn't see the cardboard boxes anywhere. He raised his hand.

"Yes?" Dr. Kirk said.

"Where are the pieces of the broken statue?" Todd asked. "I want to look at the bones again."

For just a minute Dr. Kirk seemed puzzled, then she smiled and said, "Oh, you mean the metal rods. Well, I'm afraid you can't do that."

"But we have to solve the mystery," Noelle said.

"I'm sorry. It's too late now. We're shipping the pieces back to France," Dr. Kirk said. "Willie's in the storeroom getting the boxes ready to be picked up."

"We have to look at those bones before they leave the museum," Todd whispered to Noelle.

"You're right," Noelle said.

"Oh, dear!" Dr. Kirk said.

"What's wrong?" Mr. Merlin asked.

"We're almost out of plaster. I thought I checked the stock," Dr. Kirk said. "Well, I'll just send Willie to the store to get some more."

Dr. Kirk went to the phone and dialed a number. She talked for a couple of minutes and then hung up.

"Willie won't be gone long," she said. "While

we're waiting, I'll explain to you what we're going to do."

Mr. Merlin walked up to Todd and Noelle. He put a piece of paper on the table in front of them.

"If you still want to solve this mystery, then here's a secret code clue to help you," he whispered.

Before Todd could say anything, Mr. Merlin walked away.

Todd turned to Noelle. "Mr. Merlin has never done anything like *that* before," he whispered. "He must really want us to solve this mystery fast. We haven't even *looked* at the bones yet."

Todd picked up the piece of paper.

Mr. Merlin had written:

```
L  E  g  i  N  E  v  e  R  Y
t  I  M  E  h  O  L  D  B  e
m  E  L  e  t  A  T  a  l  L
S  a  M  E  A  t  B  e  s  t
```

"We'll pretend we're getting ready to make our plaster statues, Noelle," Todd said, "but we'll really work on the secret code clue instead!"

Chapter Nine

Dr. Kirk told the Third-Grade Detectives how to get the molds ready in order to pour the plaster.

She also told them where to put the small metal rods to use for the bones.

Todd and Noelle pretended to follow her directions.

"Why doesn't Mr. Merlin just tell us what the secret code clue says?" Noelle asked. "That would save a lot of time."

"Mr. Merlin wants *us* to solve the mystery," Todd reminded her. "If he told us everything, then we wouldn't be the Third-Grade *Detectives.*"

"Okay. This sort of looks like the last secret code clue," Noelle said. "What do the capital letters spell?"

"LENERY, IMEOLDB, ELATL, SMEAB," Todd said. "Those aren't any words I know."

"Maybe this time Mr. Merlin really *does* want us to rearrange all the words we see," Noelle said. "There's 'leg,' 'in,' 'every,' 'time,' 'hold,' 'be,' 'me,' 'let,' 'at,' 'all,' 'same,' 'at,' and 'best.'"

For the next few minutes Todd and Noelle tried every possible order, but they couldn't come up with any sentences that made sense.

"If we don't hurry, Willie will be back, and we'll never get to look in those boxes," Noelle said. "Maybe we should ask Mr. Merlin for a hint."

"Wait, Noelle! I think I've got it! It's just the *opposite* of the first secret code clue," Todd said. "It's the *lowercase* letters that spell the words we need to read."

Noelle looked at the lowercase letters. *"Give the metal a test,"* she said. She looked puzzled. "How will that help us solve the mystery?"

Todd shrugged. "But if Mr. Merlin wants us to test it, then that's what we should do," he said.

"Well, come on. Let's go get a sample," Noelle said. "When we get back home, we can take it to Dr. Smiley's crime lab."

"Wait a minute," Todd told her. "One of us probably needs to stay here and pretend to work on the plaster statue.

"For some reason, I don't think Dr. Kirk really wants us to look at those bones again.

"If she sees that we're both gone, she might get suspicious.

"Maybe I'd better go by myself."

"What if Dr. Kirk asks me where you are?" Noelle said. "What should I tell her?"

"That I got sick to my stomach and had to leave," Todd said. "But make sure she doesn't come check on me."

"Okay," Noelle said.

When Dr. Kirk turned to help Misty with her plaster mold, Todd slipped out of the classroom.

He headed toward the storeroom. When he got there, it was really dark inside. Todd looked around for a light switch and finally found one.

The boxes with the parts of the broken statue were on a long table at the back. Two of them had already been taped up for shipping.

That left two for Todd to search.

He just hoped that one of the boxes had parts

of the statue with some of the metal bones in them.

Todd looked in the first box.

There were only pieces of plaster inside.

He looked in the second box.

It had the statue's head in it. A metal rod was sticking out of the neck. Todd pulled on the rod, but it wouldn't budge. Suddenly he had an idea.

He decided he would scrape off as much of the metal as he could.

Todd didn't think Dr. Smiley would need a whole lot of it to test in her lab.

He looked around for something sharp.

He didn't see anything. *What am I going to do?* he wondered. *Willie will be back any minute.*

Just then Todd remembered how he had used a coin to scrape off the silver paint from a scratch-off game piece.

He could probably use a coin to scrape off some of the metal. He pulled a quarter out of his pocket and looked around for something to put the scrapings in.

He saw a small brown envelope on a desk and hurried over and got it.

Then he held the envelope under the metal rod and started scraping. The metal shavings fell into the envelope.

Todd continued to scrape back and forth until he thought he finally had enough.

Todd closed the envelope and put it and the quarter into his pocket.

Just as he started to leave the storeroom, the door opened.

It was Willie!

"Why are you snooping around in here?" Willie demanded. He started toward Todd. "Are you trying to make trouble for us?"

"No, sir," Todd said. "I just wanted to look at the broken statue again, so I could make mine like it."

With that, Todd raced past Willie before the janitor could say anything else.

He headed back to the classroom. Just as he reached the door, he stopped.

Dr. Smiley was standing at Todd and Noelle's table with Mr. Merlin. Noelle was talking to them.

When Todd walked up, Mr. Merlin said, "There you are! I was getting worried!"

"I'm fine . . . *now,*" Todd said.

"Dr. Smiley finished her work early, so she drove over to see how we were doing," Noelle said. "Did you get any of the metal from the bones?" she whispered.

"Yes!" Todd whispered back. He looked at Dr. Smiley. "When we're back home, we need to test it in your lab," he said.

Noelle shook her head. "There's been a change of plans, Todd," she said. "Mr. Merlin said the test can't wait."

Todd looked surprised. *"Really?"* he said.

Dr. Smiley nodded. "A friend of mine is in charge of the local crime lab," she said. "I called her and told her what we needed to do. She's waiting for us."

Todd patted the pocket where he had hidden the brown envelope. "Then let's go!" he said.

Chapter Ten

"You two are really good detectives," Dr. Smiley said.

She, Todd, and Noelle were walking toward her car in the museum's parking lot.

"Thank you," Todd said.

"Is this town's crime lab as good as yours?" Noelle asked.

"It's better," Dr. Smiley said. "It's bigger and has all the equipment we'll need to do the test."

"I hope I got enough metal," Todd said. "I used a quarter to scrape it off."

"That's good to know," Dr. Smiley said. "If some of the metal from the quarter is in the sample, we can ignore that."

Dr. Smiley drove to police headquarters. She

parked her car, and they went inside. The crime lab was at the end of the hall.

Todd thought it looked like the one in his favorite TV show.

A woman in a white lab coat was standing in front of a big silver machine.

She waved to them. "Dr. Smiley!" she called. "We'll do the test here."

When they reached the woman, Dr. Smiley said, "Todd, Noelle, this is Dr. Johnson. She's the head of the crime lab. She knows everything there is to know about metals."

Dr. Johnson shook hands with Todd and Noelle.

"I understand the stolen statue was made in Orléans, France, in 1456, and that it was on loan from an art museum in Paris," Dr. Johnson said. "Is that correct?"

Todd nodded.

"Well, if you have the sample from the metal rod that was inside the statue, the machine is all ready to do the test," Dr. Johnson said.

Todd handed Dr. Johnson the brown envelope.

Dr. Johnson poured the metal shavings into a container. The machine made a whirring sound and some lights came on.

After several minutes a piece of paper scrolled out one side. Dr. Johnson tore it off.

"Well, well, well!" she said. She handed Dr. Smiley the piece of paper. "What do you think?"

Dr. Smiley read the piece of paper. "This is odd," she said. "I think we all need to go back to the museum and tell Dr. Kirk what this says."

"Could we have a meeting of the Third-Grade Detectives first?" Todd asked. "We always work together, so I want them to know why we couldn't this time."

"That sounds like a good idea, Todd," Dr. Smiley said. She took out her cell phone. "I'll call Mr. Merlin and tell him that's what we want to do."

On the way out of the building, Dr. Johnson stopped by the police chief's office.

"You need to come with us to the art museum," Dr. Johnson told her. "We've discovered something very strange about the statue that was stolen."

"All right," the chief said.

They all left police headquarters.

Dr. Johnson rode with the police chief in her patrol car. Dr. Smiley followed them with Todd and Noelle in her car.

When they reached the art museum, they went inside.

Mr. Merlin and the rest of Third-Grade Detectives were sitting together in a lounge just inside the building.

Todd and Noelle walked up to them.

"Mr. Merlin likes for us to work together to solve mysteries," Todd told them, "but we couldn't do that this time. We had to get the evidence fast and then take it to the crime lab.

"But I wanted the rest of the Third-Grade Detectives to know what happened before anybody else found out."

Todd told them about Mr. Merlin's second secret code clue.

He told them about scraping off the metal and putting it in a brown envelope, and how Dr. Johnson had used a big machine to test it.

"Now Dr. Johnson is going to tell Dr. Kirk

and Willie what the results are," Todd said.

"Dr. Kirk and Willie are still in the class-room," Mr. Merlin said. "They're putting all the statue molds on a shelf so the plaster can harden."

Everyone headed to the classroom.

When the police chief opened the door, Dr. Kirk and Willie got strange looks on their faces.

"Well, Chief, to what do we owe the pleasure of this visit?" Dr. Kirk said.

"Dr. Johnson has some information to give you," the chief said. "I think you'll find it inter-esting."

Dr. Johnson told them about Todd's evidence. "I analyzed it at the crime lab," she said.

"The metal used in that statue was made by a process not discovered until the 1900s. That statue is a fake. It wasn't made in 1456 in Orléans, France."

Dr. Kirk turned to Willie. "I told you it wouldn't work this time!" she shouted angrily.

Todd and Noelle looked at each other.

"Well, it would have if it hadn't been for the Third-Grade Detectives!" Willie shouted back.

"Would you two care to explain what you mean?" Mr. Merlin said.

"I'm not talking," Willie said. He sat down in a chair and started pouting.

But Dr. Kirk said, "Well, I am. I'll tell you everything."

It turned out, Willie wasn't really a janitor. He was actually Dr. Kirk's husband. Together, they figured out ways to steal statues from museums and sell them for lots of money to crooked art dealers.

Dr. Kirk knew a lot of museum directors around the world. She charmed them into lending their statues to her.

She and Willie then made duplicates. After that, they broke the fake statues into a lot of pieces so they couldn't be recognized. They sent the pieces back to the museum directors to keep the insurance companies from getting suspicious.

"Why would they be suspicious?" Todd asked.

"If we told them that the statue just disappeared, they might not believe us," Dr. Kirk said. "If we sent them back the pieces, they were satisfied."

"Well, *I'm* satisfied that you two have stolen your last statue," the police chief said.

She put handcuffs on Dr. Kirk and Willie and took them to jail.

On the way back to their town, Todd said, "Mr. Merlin, I saw you give Dr. Smiley a funny look when Dr. Kirk was first talking about the robbery. What were you thinking?"

Mr. Merlin smiled. "I was thinking it was strange that a janitor was telling the museum director what to do," he said.

Todd was glad they had finally solved this case. He really liked art mysteries. *You never can tell,* he thought. *One of these days I really might just be a museum director—*and *a detective!*

Whose Skull Was This?

When skeletons are found at the scene of a crime, they can give the police a lot of information. It's the job of a *forensic anthropologist* to make these skeletons "talk." The bones can tell if they belonged to a boy, a girl, a man, or a woman; the age of the person; how tall that person was; if that person had any diseases or injuries when he or she was alive; and what caused that person's death.

In addition, a *forensic sculptor* can use the skull to recreate what the person actually looked like when he or she was alive, but this takes both the objectivity of a forensic anthropologist and the creative flair of an artist.

The following activity will show you what's involved when a forensic sculptor tries to reconstruct a person's face with clay. Here's what you'll need:

1. A large plastic skull from a craft or hobby shop—the bigger, the better. These are especially easy to find around Halloween. If you can find a skull that's attached to a metal base, buy it!
2. Flesh-colored molding clay from a craft or hobby shop.

Most forensic sculptors know the depth of the tissue that covers every part of a skull. They attach little pegs around the skull, which will show them where the clay should be thick and where it should be thin. The sculptor then applies layers of clay "muscle" between the pegs. After that, the sculptor starts on the eyes, nose, mouth, ears, chin, and jowls. The width of the nose is roughly the same as the distance between the inner corners of the eyes. The corners of the mouth lie directly below the inner borders of the irises of the eyes and over the back edge of the canine teeth. The ears are roughly equal to the nose in length.

This can get kind of complicated, though, so when you're doing this project, the simplest way is just to feel your own face to see where the skin is thick and where the skin is thin. Then apply the clay accordingly. Your goal is to make your face look as lifelike as possible. When you've finished applying all of the clay, smooth it out so that it looks like skin, and then you can add either clay "hair" or a wig. If you want to, you can also add color to the eyes and the lips.

The final thing you should do is ask yourself this question: "Does this person look like anybody I know?"

Beware the hare!

" . . . *Bunnicula* is the kind of story that does not age, and in all probability, will never die. Or stay dead, anyway. . . ."
—Neil Gaiman, Newbery Medal winner

Enjoy the very best first chapter book fiction in Ready-for-Chapters books from Aladdin Paperbacks.

☐ *Jake Drake, Bully Buster*
by Andrew Clements

☐ *Annabel the Actress Starring in Gorilla My Dreams*
by Ellen Conford

☐ *The Bears on Hemlock Mountain*
by Alice Dalgliesh

☐ *The Courage of Sarah Noble*
by Alice Dalgliesh

☐ *The Girl with 500 Middle Names*
by Margaret Peterson Haddix

☐ *The Werewolf Club*
#1 The Magic Pretzel
by Daniel Pinkwater

☐ *The Werewolf Club*
#2 The Lunchroom of Doom
by Daniel Pinkwater

☐ *The Werewolf Club*
#3 The Werewolf Club Meets Dorkula
by Daniel Pinkwater

☐ *The Cobble Street Cousins*
#1 In Aunt Lucy's Kitchen
by Cynthia Rylant

☐ *The Cobble Street Cousins*
#2 A Little Shopping
by Cynthia Rylant

☐ *The Cobble Street Cousins*
#3 Special Gifts
by Cynthia Rylant

☐ *Third-Grade Detectives*
#1 The Clue of the Left-Handed Envelope
by George Edward Stanley

☐ *Third-Grade Detectives*
#2 The Puzzle of the Pretty Pink Handkerchief
by George Edward Stanley

☐ *Third-Grade Detectives*
#3 The Mystery of the Hairy Tomatoes
by George Edward Stanley

Aladdin Paperbacks

Simon & Schuster Children's Publishing • www.SimonSaysKids.com

SECRET FILES

THE HARDY BOYS®

Follow the trail with Frank and Joe Hardy in this chapter book mystery series!

BY FRANKLIN W. DIXON

FROM ALADDIN • EBOOK EDITIONS ALSO AVAILABLE

KIDS.SIMONANDSCHUSTER.COM